SCARY SHORTS

A Collection of Scary Short Stories
By Richard A. Hazard

SCARY SHORTS

First edition. February 27, 2024.

Copyright © 2024 Richard A Hazard.

ISBN: 979-8224861644

Written by Richard A Hazard.

CONTENTS

Vampire

The shadows are protection
Even the moonlight betrays us
A thirst growing in anticipation
Gender, race, or religion isn't what it's about
Your blood is red and makes us whole
A morsel of all nourishes us; there is no doubt
We are not all like vampires of old
There are variations of all monsters these days
Mostly derived from unhappy, unpleasant humans
Self-absorbed creatures, either loners or strays
Yet deadly to those who cross within their bite
Most want to feed to live
Others are seeking to devour everything in sight.

UNDER THE VEIL

I remember my wedding day as if it were yesterday. Of all the days of my life, it was the best and worst. After a wonderful ceremony, we were on our way to a quaint little bed and breakfast in Santa Barbara for our honeymoon. In the passenger seat of our rental, Maria looked like a blossoming rose.

"Rafael, look out!" Maria screamed.

There was no time to react; we collided with a delivery truck, ending our marvelous wedding day in my new wife's death. Her airbag opened with such force that it snapped her neck like a dry wishbone from the Thanksgiving Turkey. She was pronounced dead on arrival.

Maria looked ravishing as she was laid to rest in her wedding dress. I asked that she be buried with her veil covering her face so death wouldn't be able to see the beauty it stole from me.

As the days passed into weeks, my heart sank to new depths of sorrow, I hadn't believed humanly possible. It was in one of those sinking moments in which I thrust a butcher knife into my chest.

Later, I awoke in a room filled with flowers and dim lighting. Muted tones of peaceful music were playing from hidden speakers. There was a slight smell of death in the room, which was barely noticeable through the fragrance of freshly cut blooms.

My body felt restricted within what appeared to be a box at first. Yet I could move my fingers and toes without any difficulty. A sudden flash of reality engulfed me when I remembered the last few moments of my former life. So, my box was a coffin ready for my final performance in the world of the living.

Wishing to escape life, I chose death only to awake in my coffin alive, or so it seemed. Puzzlement wasn't the only thing I felt; a bitter cold was biting at my chest.

"How can I be alive without blood?" I asked myself. Though I was never a mortician, I knew they replaced blood with embalming fluid. At least in the flicks I had seen. Rolling out of the coffin onto the floor, then clumsily pulling myself up. I steadied my legs and looked around to see that I was in the same mortuary Maria had been in.

Slowly, I walked towards the door. Just a step before I was going to leave the room, I looked back to where my body had rested. My mouth fell open as I watched my corpse gradually vanish before my eyes.

Lifting my hand in front of my eyes, I could see it, though not clearly. A sudden pain wrenched my side, dropping me to my knees. With one fluid movement, I ripped open my shirt and stared in disbelief as the stitches in my chest tore, releasing the newly acquired fluids my body held.

Thirsty, I became aware of my great thirst and desire to get warmth for my chilling body. Weakness overwhelmed me as I struggled to stand and walk to the door. Then the mortician stopped me in my tracks. She walked through me towards my last known resting place, then screamed. I'm sure the sight of an empty coffin was a bit hard to swallow. Yet, it was a wonder she hadn't seen me.

My body felt every cell as she passed through effortlessly. Her scent lingered in my nostrils even after she left to call the police. Lust engulfed me, and I knew I wanted to take her in my arms and kiss her, imagining she was my Maria. I also wanted her blood to surge through my empty veins. My overwhelming thirst for blood is consuming me.

Finally, there was a reason to keep on living, even in my current form. The police would come and go, baffled by what they couldn't find, mainly a body. They would be scratching their heads as they left, my prey alone and vulnerable. I knew once I had her life in my veins, the cold would end. My every instinct assured me of that.

While the police investigated, I had a few hours to experiment with my new body, trying to find its new abilities and limitations.

No one else could see me, yet I could see myself. Walls were no longer obstacles that had to be walked around. I merely cleared my mind as I started walking forward and then passed through.

Touching my hand to a doorknob, I would let my hand join with the knob, becoming one. Then, through sheer will, turned, pushed, and presto, the door would open.

I didn't have to wait long before she turned out the lights and locked the doors. I could smell her blood from across the room, from where I now stood. With every beat of her heart, and the flow in her veins, a raging tide of life. I believed myself ready for a warm drink of blood and the love stolen from me by death. Slowly, I walked towards the women who would quench my thirst and refill me with life's ebb.

Without a second's hesitation, I grabbed each of her hands in my own, letting them join. We were now one. Forcing her onto her back, she hit her head firmly on the concrete. She lay unconscious, helpless against my assault.

For the first time, I looked at her face. Her light caramel colored skin, black curly hair, and perky lips captivated me further. I wouldn't wait any longer.

I undressed her as well as myself and started to make love as I imagined it would have been with my Maria. There was no returned passion or hot and heavy kissing. A one-sided encounter as I gradually kissed my way up her stomach to her throat.

Beneath the skin of her neck pulsed the nectar which I craved. With one fatal plunge, I bit through the neck into the artery, drinking from her fountain of warm blood. Gradually, the woman stopped breathing, and her body turned cold.

Energy surged through my body, tingling with the flow of blood, traveling in rivers of blood vessels. The impulse to scratch took over my left hand, which immediately met with a scab on my chest. I looked to where there had been an open wound minutes before to see a large scab in its place. With a single swipe of my fingernail, the crumbly covering fell to the ground next to the lifeless body of the woman I had just killed.

What had I become? Was there a reason to live? Now, after I was warm and full of strength, I wasn't so sure. Guilt riddled my soul with anguish. Now, instead of death, I would live, live.

I'm alive, and the woman I love is dead and buried. A Marriage that was to bind us as one has separated us forever. If only she could have gone through the same kind of metamorphosis as I did, we could still be together.

With my last thought coaxing me, I hurriedly dressed and ran through the wall to the street. Since the cemetery was only a couple of blocks away, I would know in a brief time whether she was indeed alive. First, I needed to take a little trip to the hospital and top off with a bit more blood, any type, positive or negative. After a short hour and two pints of blood, I was finally on my way to my beloved's resting place.

Maria's unmarked grave stopped me short. The flowers I laid on her grave just a week before were wilted and turning brown. With nothing to lose and my bride to gain, I cleared my mind and plunged headfirst into my dead wife's grave.

Once I started in the coffin, I was stopped abruptly by something I didn't know. The darkness prevailed even after my eyes were open. My wife's hand clinched mine, and a surge of electricity tingled my body.

"Why are you still here, my love?"

"I was just waiting for you to come. What kept you? Did another lover detain you?" Immediately, I was ashamed of my infidelity. At once, I decided not to say a word. How would she ever find out?

"Maria, why are you so cold?"

"I thirst for blood. Blood drained from me at the mortuary. Take me out of here and find a suitable donor for my replenishing."

Without delay, I pulled her out of the grave and took her in my arms. She was cold to the point of shivering. My Maria needed blood even more desperately than I had. So, we headed to the one-stop shop, the hospital was nearly empty but full of blood. There was no reason to kill again; there were always alternatives. Besides, I couldn't get the mortician's lifeless body out of my head.

Maria drank eight pints of blood before she said she was full. She had me turn my head when she lifted her veil to drink. She said I couldn't see her face again until the honeymoon resumed later in the evening. Though I wanted to see my beloved's face again, I decided to wait. My joy seemed almost complete. Except for the haunting guilt felt over the murder I committed only two hours before.

"Maria, I have to tell you something."

"You did have another woman after I died, didn't you?"

"No, I mean yes, I mean. Listen, I killed a woman earlier this evening for the blood which flowed through her veins. I was caught up in the moment and driven by a total loss of inhibitions."

"What are we, Rafael?"

"We are a type of vampire. Though I'm not entirely sure yet."

"Well, the blood I drank did seem to bring warmth and strength to my tired body. The only thing to do now is find a place to sleep or live, or whatever it is we do."

"If you don't mind looking at the woman I killed, we could stay in her apartment. It's up on the second floor of the mortuary."

"I don't think she'll mind, Rafael. Let's go."

I couldn't quite put my finger on the difference, but Maria had changed. Being dead for a few months had something to do with it.

We passed through the front doors and walked down the hall to the large room where I had killed the mortician. When we entered the room, I stopped, dropping my hands onto my sides. Words escaped me as I stood dumbfounded.

"What's wrong, Lover?"

Her sentence struck a nerve, which exasperated me further. Maria never would have said that before.

"Rafael, didn't you say you killed someone here in this room. Where did you put the body?"

"I didn't put it anywhere. There should be a nude corpse by the back doors."

"Did you say nude?"

"It doesn't matter, the body is gone." Frantically, I ran through every room and wall, searching for the missing corpse. It was gone; there wasn't a trace of it anywhere. I silently returned to Maria's side, wishing I could see under the veil, sharing the expression on her face.

"The body's gone, let's just forget about it and go to bed. I want to start the honeymoon that death stole from us."

Taking me by the hand, Maria led me up the stairs to the second floor. I told her to take a left at the top of the stairway and go to the last door. Even with my directions, she already seemed to know where we were headed. Entering the room, Maria undressed, taking off everything but her veil.

I quickly undressed and turned down the bed. Slowly, she walked towards me in the light of a full moon. In the distance, I heard a dog bark a couple of times, then there was only silence. The night seemed to be entertaining our moment.

Maria sat on my stomach, her veil still covering her lovely face. She asked if I still loved her. Silently, she waited for an answer.

"Of course, I do. There could never be another woman for me."

"Do you take this bride to be your wife, for better or for worse?"

"I do." I felt silly answering, but decided to play along. "Do you take this groom, for better or for worse?"

"I do." There was a short pause before she spoke again. "You may now kiss the bride." She drew near my face and lifted the veil, but the shadows kept me from seeing her face. We kissed passionately for several minutes.

I never wanted the moment to end. Finally, everything was the way it was supposed to be. Maria and I were wed and together forever.

Suddenly, she sat up and grabbed my hands very tightly. In the moonlight, I finally saw her face. I screamed in horror when I realized who I was with.

"Oh yeah, Big Boy. I took your wife's body. Of course, I like my head better than hers. The rip in my neck and hers being broken made the modification all the easier. Since we're married, let's start the honeymoon? Oh, and our love making isn't one-sided any longer."

My fate is sealed in a marriage of my design, a fitting hell for the living dead.

Werewolf

The full moon is bright
The howling roams the forest this night
Yellow eyes peering in the darkness
Sending victims to eternal blackness
Swiftly moving like the wind through the trees
Death approaches like a chilling breeze
Growling, snarling, baring wickedly sharp teeth
A deadly predator with a human beneath
Eventually returning to its true state
Until the next turning and another's fate.

BROTHERS UNDER THE MOONLIGHT

The Ranger's eyes slowly opened and adjusted to the dim light. He was lying in a large cave, which was cool but filled with a foul stench. Cord smelled rotten flesh, or was that his breath? While sliding his tongue across his upper teeth, there was no longer any doubt. Strings of meat clung between what used to be his pearly whites. The heaviness of his head increased with a flash of memory.

He had fallen. No! He was shot and fell headlong into a shallow ravine. His next memory was one of being drug by the pant legs to what he was sure was his current location. Someone was feeding him occasionally, enough to keep him alive.

He seemed to remember voices; they were spoken to him, but he didn't understand everything they said. Cord gingerly felt for the wound in his side. His fingers

instinctively found their mark, but what he felt was a thick mound of fur.

"What the hell?" Cord spoke aloud.

"Quiet, the hunters are still looking for your body."

Cord didn't hear the voice; he saw them in his mind. He thought he was going crazy. No, he had died, and this was his hell.

"You are alive, but your death was here and left without taking your body. We must wait to see about your soul." Again, the words flashed through his head.

"Who are you? Show yourself."

A grizzled gray wolf walked from the shadows of the cave. This was one of the largest gray wolves Cord had ever seen. Though it was painful, Cord sat up and scooted to the wall opposite the huge beast before him. He was sure that this wolf was over six feet long from nose to tail, with a height of at least three feet.

Though the wolf didn't say a word, Cord knew what he was saying. The weirdest part of what Cord was feeling was the feeling of being in the same room with his father.

"The men who knocked you down with the flying weapon are still in the area. They look for you."

"I caught them hunting in the preserve, and they didn't like the thought of going to jail." Cord said aloud. Then he wondered why he even spoke to the gray wolf before him.

"You speak to me out of the respect any pup has for its parent." Then the wolf growled and walked back to the entrance and out of the lair. Cord knew wolves rarely attacked humans, but that didn't mean he was safe in a cave with God knows how many wolves.

"Pup! A Wolf Scowled. "Rest, by tomorrow you will be strong enough to wander from here on your own. Right now, it's time to feed and sleep." The wolf's words were those of a concerned mother. How did he know that?

Cord lay back, closing his eyes. He awoke later in the evening to the report of a single rifle. Though it seemed distant, he was worried. There were numerous species of wildlife left unprotected while he lay in a cave deep within the forest.

His anger was culminating within. The back of his legs started to tremble at the thought of hunters ruining the atmosphere of the preserve. A severe pain tore at his side, and he howled in pain. Twisting in spasms, he stood quickly, trying to work out the charley horse in his left leg.

Another howl, then a deep growl backed up the other wolves in the lair, and Cord walked towards the entrance on all fours. Once outside, Cord lifted his nose in the air and sniffed in search of a particular scent.

After a few attempts, he could distinguish the faint smell of gunpowder from that of bear and squirrel. Also in the mix were scents of pine and dogwood trees. Cord left the lair at a full gait in the direction of the enemy. His dark gray coat was thick from tail to head, except for a small patch of furless skin underneath the right side of his belly. The night posed no problem for his yellow-tinted eyes. He heard the poachers laughing about the bear they had killed only minutes before. They wouldn't be laughing for long.

When the large Gray Wolf neared the wood line, which was just fifteen feet from the humans, he stopped. He knew the three men by sight. They were the same ones who hunted him down like an animal after destroying their traps.

"Brenner will be back in the morning," said the burly beer-bellied lout.

"Yeah, he's reporting the missing ranger. You know how he tried to help, but the Ranger fell off the cliff into the Kantishila River and is floating downstream. That should buy us enough time to finish collecting our traps and high tail it out of here." The skinny man with the fuzzy beard stood and walked out of the firelight and into the woods. "I'll be back in a few. Mother Nature's calling."

"You won't be back at all; I'll make sure of it." Cord thought as he walked in a circle to come behind the thin man. The man was too engrossed in how far he could tinkle to be alert enough to hear Cord walk up. A deep growl reverberated from the wolf's mouth, startling the skinny man, who turned quickly.

In a single leap, the Gray Wolf was atop the poacher, with teeth bared for the kill. Only a few seconds were needed for Cord to rip the throat out. Then the quick altercation was over, and the Gray Wolf marked his territory by hiking his right rear leg over the dead body.

Cord heard the other two humans approaching, so he walked off quietly towards a denser area of forest. He wouldn't journey far; Cord wanted to stay within the sound of their voices.

"Look, Will! Look at the size of that wolf."

"I see it, Kurt, but I don't believe it." After a few more shaky steps, Kurt screamed, "My God!"

The other poacher shone his flashlight in front of himself and froze. Kurt saw the shine of wet blood and bent over, grabbing his stomach. He proceeded to upchuck his previous two meals.

"If it weren't bad enough seeing Lucky with his throat and innards strung all over his body, you got to go and puke on my boot. That's it! I know which way the wolf went, so I'll just pick up my rifle and get on my way to killing the beast." Will started towards the camp with a quick canter.

"What am I supposed to do?" yelled Kurt.

Without stopping, Will blurted, "Go get Brenner and meet me right here in the morning."

"Man, I told Lucky and Will not to shoot the pup yesterday. This whole thing gives me the creeps." Kurt talked to himself as he made his way to the old pickup. He turned before he climbed into the Ford as if he knew someone or something was staring at him. Fumbling for the right key, Kurt finally started the truck and sped away as fast as was possible.

As Cord slowly walked behind the poacher called Will, he started having a flashback of his wolf parents giving him life. Their pup just gave his last breath and lay motionless on the cave floor. The Alpha male ripped a good-sized chunk of fur and skin from the corpse and stuffed it in Cord's wound to stop the bleeding.

The Alpha female tore meat from the hole in the pup's side and chewed it. After several seconds of tenderizing, she dropped the food into Cord's mouth for him to eat. Somehow, what the wolves did changed him. Did they know? "So, you killed the pup that gave me life, and this altered state. Well, let's dispose of another killer brother. There's a full moon out and I feel great."

Brenner and Kurt arrived the next morning at a lifeless camp. The fire had long gone out, and a stench of urine overwelled the entire area.

Brenner was a heavy man with a thick beard and a crooked nose. By its looks, it must have been flattened more than once. The smell was sickening, and he choked a bit. He pulled a handkerchief from his pocket to cover his nose and mouth.

"Where's Lucky's body?" Brenner asked a bit muffled.

"Follow me," said Kurt. He didn't hesitate to show the whereabouts of the dead man. His pace was quick until he reached the place where Lucky's fly-covered body lay. That's

when Kurt bent over and spewed again.

Behind and to the left of the first dead body were the remains of what was Will. He was dismembered but arranged in a neat single pile. The stench of urine was strong, even overpowering the smell of Lucky's rotting flesh.

Cord followed the faded blue pickup to the camp at a great distance. He would wait for the perfect opportunity to rid the world of Brenner. He watched from deep within the forest as Brenner and Kurt buried the bodies and tore down the camp. Kurt was a whiner, and Brenner a bully.

Cord hated men who came into federal parks and reserves to hunt animals the government was eagerly trying to preserve. The Gray Wolf was scarcely found anywhere else in the United States, and here were a few idiots taking pot shots at wolf pups barely weaned.

Becoming fervently filled with rage, Cord howled deeply, for the forest would share his anger. Then he sat down to listen to the human trash converse.

"That's the monster, he's going to get us next," screamed Kurt.

"Shut up, sissy. One wolf isn't going to do any harm. Now let's finish up and get the hell out of here." Brenner felt a pit in his large stomach tugging at his cowardice. The trip hadn't gone right from the start.

First, that nosy Ranger found some traps, and Will killed him. Then Lucky and Will played a little target practice with the wolf pup. Neither body ever recovered. He'd poached for nearly fifteen years but had never seen anything like what he'd seen in the camp when he arrived.

Suddenly, the afternoon silence erupted into a chorus of howls which seemed to come from every direction. Brenner heard a scuffling noise to his right and turned to see Kurt running for the ford. Brenner knew better than to act scared or try to run.

Kurt made it to the truck, rolled up the windows and locked the doors. He pulled his feet underneath his butt and watched the wolves emerge from the tree line, surrounding both himself and Brenner.

The truck was hit by something, which bounced with tremendous force. A flash of dark gray hopped from the back of the truck bed onto the hood and down to the ground. Kurt's mouth dropped open, and he peed his pants at the sight of a giant wolf. A wolf half a size larger than the ones encircling the camp.

Cord stood between his wolf parents and Brenner, his eyes aglow with beastly emotions surging through his veins. He spoke softly with mental words. "Kill the leader, have your revenge. But the one in the truck is to live and be punished by human law. Some humans care about us. Please keep him here until I return." With no more than a turn of the head, his new parents agreed.

Cord ran full tilt to the ranger station a couple of miles to the east. Slowing once to hear the screams of Brenner's fleeting life. Once he entered his home, he slowly turned back to his human form, showered, dressed, and returned in his jeep to the poacher's camp.

He pulled up behind the faded truck, turned off the engine, and walked towards the last killer. His wolf family was content and still, sitting in a circle, keeping guard. As Cord rounded the front of the Ford, he noticed there wasn't much of Brenner's body to dispose of. Of course, Kurt was yelling inside the truck.

"Get out of there or they'll tear you apart. Ranger, your dead get out of here."

The wolves turned, leaving as one and disappearing into the forest. The ranger opened the door and grabbed Kurt by the arm, hauling him out of the vehicle. "Remember me!"

"I'm glad you're alive, man, I'm glad you showed up, I just knew I was a goner."

Cord allowed his head to change to his altered state, and he growled while his nose touched that of Kurt's.

Cord dropped the man who fell in a slump, peeing himself and begging for life. Then, turning back to full human form, he picked Kurt from the ground. Cuffing and tossing him back in the truck. Cord would deal with the last poacher the human way. Before driving away, Cord stopped to listen to his forest.

The birds began to chirp from high in the trees, and his wolf father howled. "Who better to protect the forest than one who is bound to the forest. Death passed by your soul, son."

Gargoyle

Protectors
High above and looking down
Adorning the tops of buildings
Keeping out the demons
Though they are called demons
Stone by day
Flesh by night
Alive
Guardians of the innocent
Yellow eyes piercing the darkness
Of both night and the human soul
A row of razor-sharp teeth
Claws for piercing
Bringing evil to its demise
All in a night's work
Again, resting on their silent perches.

LIVING MEGALITH

My withered body trembled as blood surged through dead veins again. Though my corpse had shriveled some, the seal of cement had preserved me during my time of imprisonment. Sentenced to death by a greedy lowlife son-of-a-b—-.

Paretti had built a huge mansion with a garden maze. In the center of this maze, he wanted a miniature Stonehenge. I was happy to help him design and build the half-sized MEGALITH model. A miniature Stonehenge in a garden would be quite an accomplishment.

After designing and constructing the molds for the half-sized model, I found out some of the original sarsen stones from England were being ground into powder and mixed with the cement being poured into the molds.

My arguments to stop the construction were met with fatal resistance. Toothless Magerk held me while Heavy forced handfuls of the cement mixture into my mouth, eventually dropping me in one of the molds. Unable to breathe, I died in a cement tomb of my design. Until today, my last memory was one of cement being poured over my entire body, engulfing me.

I awoke suddenly as the ground began to tremble, shaking the stone which had become my final resting place. It fell crashing backwards or forwards, I'm not sure which. Pieces of rock shattered from my body, letting me escape from my prison. Immediately, I stumbled to my feet and awkwardly walked into the shadows.

Feeling a strength impossibly surging through my body, after all, I had been dead. How long had I been entombed? My torn clothes fell from my growing body. Originally 5.9, surely now at least seven feet. Suddenly, my back ripped open, and wings emerged. My new wings are reminiscent of dragon-shaped wings. What had I become? My new wings stretched out and then merged onto my back as if they were not there at all.

I had to find a place to live hidden away from the world.

A place Paretti wouldn't think of looking. Then I remembered the Two-Mile Crib was supposed to be decommissioned in 1933. I hope these wings work, as they say the shortest distance is a straight line. They instinctively opened, and with a leap, I was off and on my way to what I hoped would be a vacant home.

The Crib had been used to bring fresh lake water into Chicago. Outliving its usefulness it was being replaced by a newer model.

So, it's closed, which means I've been dead at least a year. Hopefully not much longer. The longer it has been, the stronger Paretti will have become. Entering from a door in the roof, I made my way into the abandoned building. There was no problem with my sight in the confines of darkness. Everything within the room was visible with little effort.

"What had I become? What had Paretti turned me into?" The structure had everything needed to live except for food, which I wasn't sure I needed anyway.

"Now, it would be my home." If there were a mirror above the sink in the water closet, I could see what I had become. With anxiety and excitement growing with every step, I made my way into what would bring me to my new truth.

The features that had been Jack Wright were no longer recognizable. The creature before me was only human in that it stood upright and was endowed with the right plumbing. I was naked and light gray. Every angle blocked and chiseled, a masterpiece if I were made as a monument to be set on a stoop at City Hall.

The hairless being before me was a stranger to my eyes, yet familiar to my feelings. I believed my skin and cells had been mutated by the fragments of the real Stonehenge ingested with the cement. Without any true scientific knowledge, there was no doubt this would be my permanent form. Only able to prowl at night from roof to roof, flying and trying to stay in the shadows.

Yes, it was too late for me, but there were other innocents whom Paretti would victimize. I would no longer go by the name Jack Wright, but would be known as Megalith. A suitable name to describe the rigid, stony being I had become.

Tomorrow night, I will begin to foil Paretti's plans of becoming the strongest fiercest force in the city, but for now, I will sleep.

Waking at dusk, unrested due to haunting dreams of Gargoyles flying down on my body and carrying me away to an unknown destination. All of them had Paretti's face and uppity laugh. They dropped me to the ground hundreds of feet above, and I awoke just before impact.

The strength throughout my entire body was new to me. My first glimmer of this untested muscle was manifested when I leapt from the rooftop of the building I inhabited. The jump was effortless and invigorating. Of course, why jump when you can fly?

My first stop would be Paretti's mansion. There, I would be able to find out some of his plans and play a little havoc with his boys. I hadn't forgotten Toothless Mcgerk and Heavy, they should be rewarded for what they put me through.

The trip across town took less than ten minutes as a Gargoyle flies. Paretti's mansion couldn't be missed. I saw it a mile away with its windows brightly lit by enormous crystal chandeliers. Visible from my vantage point. My old grave was cleaned up, but the stone had not been replaced yet. The driveway was bumper to bumper with black Tudors and Victorias. Paretti only bought Fords for his men to drive.

Slowly, I worked my way around the grounds until I was just behind the collapsed miniature Stonehenge, which was my prison until the night before. The ruins were being watched by two of Paretti's henchmen, who were walking back and forth between the mansion and the fallen stones.

From what I remembered, gangsters were good thugs or enforcers, but lousy guards. The breed of men who normally enter the family was too nervous to have patience as a character trait.

Not more than fifteen minutes later, the short wait paid off. The heavier of the two hoodlums stopped at the corner of the building to roll a cigarette. The tall, hawk-faced thug quickly joined his partner for a much-needed break.

When they turned their backs to block the wind from blowing out their matches, I jumped to the tallest part of the ruins. Then, without any hesitation, I jumped onto the roof of the mansion just above the guards. There, my landing was far from perfect, and I rolled a good ten feet, waiting motionless as the two guards came to life.

"Who's there?"

"It wasn't nuttin" said the hawk-faced thug.

In a few moments, the two men resumed their walk. My hearing was more acute than it had ever been. I could hear their steps. They kept walking past the fake ruins.

Now to find ways to ruin Paretti and his whole family. Though I found great advantages with my new body, I would make him pay for killing me. My thoughts constantly working out a plan of attack. How many would be destroyed in his path to becoming the wealthiest and most powerful crime boss in the Windy City?

Luckily for me, the rooftop patio was not lit tonight. I had attended parties here, and if it were lit up, I would never be able to go unnoticed. Even in the moonlight, the patio roof looked immaculate. Every tile perfectly laid, and each shrub is evenly groomed. The tables, umbrellas, and chairs were neatly stacked against the side opposite me. The way to the stairs was uninhibited.

The stairs to the center courtyard are dimly lit and guarded by roving guards. I had to make my way to the room which adjoined the conference room, there I would find out how to ruin Paretti. I heard the man long before he rounded the corner.

To lift myself out of sight, I quickly jumped up, thrusting sharp claw-shaped toes into the wall. Simultaneously reaching upwards, I dug my right fingers into the ceiling and waited with my left hand prepped for a blow to the man's head. The tall, thin man in a pinstriped suit fell in a crumpled heap after my fist hit and smashed his skull, splattering blood on the walls and floor of the surrounding room.

Slowly, I eased myself to the floor and walked around the corner to the room where I hoped to overhear information that would benefit my current cause. Their voices were clear from where I silently knelt.

"Yes, Sir, Mr. Paretti. We will take out the Highball Club tomorrow night, after the protection money has been collected."

"When?" Paretti's deep voice reverberated through the wall.

"After it's closed."

"No! During its peak hours, you will cancel their business license."

Silence lingered in the room for a long ten seconds. Then Paretti's voice once again took control. "Then the message will be clear. We give our blessings, and we take them away."

"Yes, Boss," the voice was shaky.

"Then take all the money in the joint while destroying the club. Delivering it here after midnight, make sure you don't wake me."

"So, Paretti, you're still pushing your weight around," I whispered. That was all I needed to know. Tomorrow would be the beginning of the end for Paretti's empire. First, I would thwart his plans to destroy the club, stealing his collection money as my back pay, and a mental anguish bonus. Finally, I would wake the master of the house, putting him to sleep permanently."

Dawn was approaching in a little less than an hour. So, I needed to blow the joint. Within a minute, gaining access to the roof patio. Peering over the edge, I could see the stone onto which I would jump.

Before I was able to begin my descent, a bullet ricocheted off my chest. A small drop of blood ran down my grayish colored body. Without a moment's hesitation, I jumped, flying in the opposite direction from my home.

Bullets pelted my stomach like small rocks. There was no time to slow and fight, so I just disappeared into the night sky.

When I at last reached my new home, there was time enough to check my wounds. Surprisingly, there were no holes or serious bleeding. The bleeding stopped almost immediately. Though overjoyed at my tough new skin, I had not overlooked the fact that I had indeed bled. Therefore, I was not invincible. The next morning at ten o'clock, I was waiting on the roof of the building adjoining the Highball Club. The rumble of an approaching car caught my attention. The high gloss shine of the black Tudor was the clue to who was inside. Just as I had anticipated. Thugs always seem to first attack from the darkness. Paretti's men were no exception. Then they moved from the alley to the rear of the Club.

All the men wore dark suits and brimmed hats. They walked with a swagger as though they were completely assured of their victory. Their arrogance would increase the amount of surprise they would face in death. I bounced off the top of the black sedan, then onto two of the creeps before they knew what hit them.

With a shuffle first to one side, then to the other, I put the nearest three into the hereafter with a solid backhand to their heads, snapping their necks. The lone survivor ran into the darkness of the night ranting like a madman. I let him go, turning my attention to the back door of the club.

The "Highball Club" was lit like a Christmas tree. People were dancing while a cute woman sang with a miniature version of a big band. The club was roaring with life. Life, which Paretti had no regard for. Paretti was going down, and I would reap my vengeance and my reward all in the same night.

From my roost above the stage, my field of vision was open and clear. The open areas were not where the thugs were going to attack from. No, they would be in the shadows, behind doorways, and curtains. Wouldn't they be surprised when they found themselves all alone?

My improved feline-like eyesight showed where most of the night's would-be corpses were hiding. Utilizing the same shadows as the gangsters, I eased my way down the wall behind my next kill. The three roughens that had encircled the back of the stage were dead and lying in pools of their blood within five minutes. The only killers left were the two standing by the front doors.

Though I didn't want to be seen, there was little choice. Either I made an appearance, or a lot of innocent people were going to die when the two men let loose with their tommy guns.

I escaped the darkness onto the brightly lit stage with a roar that had begun in the pit of my stomach. Whether it was my size, grotesque appearance, or just sheer surprise, I'm not sure. Both men and women screamed at the creature I had become. My plan worked, and the crowd swarmed the front doors, trampling the gangsters underfoot.

Turning to finish the job, I noticed my handiwork for the first time. Blood was still seeping from the three bodies near the back of the stage. My stomach cramped and I doubled over, puking on the floor. Now I, too, have become a murderer. But I had become a murderer of murderers.

Sirens! Now was the time to leave. Tonight, Paretti would receive his just rewards. The rooftops held my highway to the subject of my revenge.

My arrival at the mansion was only moments before the drop of the night's take. There were six thugs outside the cozy confines of Paretti's home, three of whom congregated at the ruins of the master's folly.

Instead of waiting for the perfect moment, I rushed to their positions, barreling as fast as my legs would take me. The flat-footed, hawk-faced guard from the night before was my first victim. He flew a good ten feet before hitting the side of the brick house headfirst. His skull cracked with a hollow thump. The heavier victim raised his hand, exposing a pistol. I heard the cocking of the gun echo in my ears. I took two steps towards him and felt the warmth of a slight wound open in my chest and the roar of the report.

With a kick of my left leg, my sharp, clawed foot struck the gangster in the throat, gushing blood down the front of him. He instinctively clutched his throat as he fell to the ground, gurgling.

The third man ran, throwing his piece in the air behind him. He will live to tell someone else about the monster he has seen. I was startled by a commotion within the mansion.

Many feet were on their way to this side of the house. So, I jumped to the patio and followed my route from the day before.

Paretti's voice was bellowing orders to his puppets. He would make his way to the den where he would wait for a report. I entered the den and took a seat in the oversized high-backed chair, waiting for my enemy to arrive. The desk had been elevated a foot to raise his posture in front of his men. I remembered standing there the night I was killed and feeling so insignificant. Now the one responsible would know how it feels.

Paretti entered with two thugs, each carrying four bags of money. He took the situation in immediately. He pulled his suit down to appear unwrinkled and not worried by the problem facing him. The two hardcases with him were visibly shaken. I noticed one had a pale-yellow puddle beneath his feet. I recognized him as toothless McGerk. The other thug was Heavy, a large brute of a man.

"Who are you?" asked the mob leader firmly.

"I used to be known as Jack Wright, but now, due to my rock-hardened body, you may call me Megalith. Now drop my backpay and step aside. Don't, set it in the puddle." I believe I noticed a trickle of sweat dripping down the side of his face. Yes, he was scared. I could smell the fear in him.

I sensed the nearness of the ceiling; I must appear to be a giant to the three men. The one who had earlier peed his trousers ran. The other raised his Tommy gun and let the bullets fly. A couple hit me squarely in my chest and caused me to sit back in the chair.

I left the chair in a leap, landing on the bully's head. The crack of breaking bones lasted longer than the burst of gunfire a moment before. While I was in the swing of things, I back-handed Paretti across the mouth, sending him sprawling across the room.

Again, the sounds of footsteps were nearing my location. Paretti grabbed his heater and shot into my body at point-blank range. His bullets broke the skin on my stomach, but were not of any concern to me now.

So, picking up the scum bag which had become the object of my revenge, I shook him until he fell limp. Then tossed him towards the double doors of the den as his men were breaking in. Catching them by surprise, they all fired into Paretti's body, riddling it with holes.

Without any hesitation, I grabbed the bags of money and trampled one of the men under my feet. The others opened fire with their Tommy guns. Though I felt weakened by the many cuts suffered through the night, there was no time to slow my pace. To the rooftop and on swift wings was my escape. In my weakened state, the trip seemed to take forever. The closer I got to home, the better I was feeling.

Once, back in my hideaway, I realized what I first thought would be the end of the whole affair was only the beginning. Though Paretti was dead, the family was only stymied for a short time. There would be more Jack Wrights, who would need protection. More clubs needing a warrior on their side.

Megalith would be the reckoning force of the innocent. Tomorrow to figure out how to get the mini-Stonehenge out of the family's control. So far, they didn't know how to use their powers. Hell, even I don't know that.

The Grave

The grave is not the end
A resting place for the physical portion
An entrance to eternity for the soul
Six feet below
In the stillness of the earth
Portals open to engulf the breathless
Quickening the lifeless
Unless the grave is unsealed
No headstone
No recorded day of death
If disturbed
The dead shall rise
Raining havoc on their supposed loved ones
The grave is not the end
Those we love should enter the great light
Not stuck on this earth
Send them on their one-way trip to the hereafter
Beneath a headstone exclaiming their life and death
Sealed

DEATH UNSEALED

The office door slammed, rattling windows and waking Burt from his nap. From the adjoining room, he heard Sheriff Tate carrying on a conversation with somebody. The Sheriff seemed frustrated over something that had happened. He kept repeating, "I don't want the chicken soup, it's gross."

Though Burt didn't want to interrupt the sheriff, perhaps he could help. Putting his ear to the door, the deputy was convinced the Sheriff was carrying on a conversation with himself.

"Maybe the celebration at the cemetery was more than he could handle, or maybe his cold is a bit more than a cold. Oh well, I'm talking to myself now as well." Burt tapped on the door, turning the doorknob simultaneously, as it swung open, he said. "I don't mean to interrupt, Sheriff, but is there something I can do to help?"

The deputy saw a woman leaving through the other door.

"I thought you were talking to yourself."

"No, I don't need help, and no, I wasn't talking to myself, though I might as well have been. Leave me alone, Burt." The Sheriff was shaken. He seemed pale and stood wide-eyed as he spoke to Burt.

"What's up, sheriff. You look like you've seen a ghost?"

The Sheriff took two steps forward, forcing Burt to the wall. The Sheriff's fists were clenched, and his mouth was contorted in madness.

"What did you say, O'Brien?"

"Never mind, Sheriff, shouldn't you be in bed nursing that cold?"

"I was sleeping like a baby until my wife brought me some chicken soup."

Burt smiled at the statement and reached out a hand to check the Sheriff's forehead for a temperature. The older man ducked, but Burt clamped his palm and fingers around the Sheriff's head. With a quick jerk backwards, the older man was out of arm's reach.

"I knew better than to say anything to you, Burt. You never take anything seriously. Get out of here and leave me alone."

"You are right, Al, but I'm ready to listen, if you're ready to get it off your chest. Now let's have it from the top." The Sheriff eyed him for a few seconds, then sighed and shook his head in submission. Burt noticed it was exceedingly difficult for his boss to start.

"After I went home, I lay down on the couch and fell asleep. I heard footsteps and opened my eyes to those of my dead wife. She handed me a bowl and a package of crackers. "You deserve this," she said.

"It only took one look for me to lose my breakfast and get shut out of my home."

"I want to believe you, Sheriff, but you must admit it seems a little far-fetched. After all, your wife has been dead a year, hasn't she?"

"Who do you think was leaving the office when you walked in?"

"Sheriff," I said with a chagrin expression on my face.

"I figured you might not believe me, so I brought the soup to prove my story. Here, take a look."

The deputy was handed an evidence bag full of soup. Burt looked like he expected to see chicken soup. Guts, bones, and chicken feathers were floating inside. The broth was water dyed red with blood. He dropped the bag and covered his mouth with his left hand.

The phone rang, bringing the deputy back to the moment, allowing an appreciated break. Burt started for the door to the front desk.

"I'll get the phone, Sheriff. I need to get away for a moment."

The Sheriff heard the phone ring repeatedly, and then there was silence. The deputy entered the Sheriff's office, who was gagging with a bowl of soup in his hand. "Another visit from your wife?"

The Sheriff just glared at the Deputy.

"We received five more phone calls, every one of them about ghost visits by dead relatives who were mean, even abusive. What's going on around here?"

The Sheriff, still visibly shaken by the ordeal with his wife, wasn't much help. "I'm not sure, but there seems to be a pattern. Burt, make a list of the people who have been seen. Check with the Undertaker about the people on the list."

"Oh, Al, that guy's downright spooky."

"Would you rather eat my wife's soup?"

"I'm gone." Burt parked in front of the old theater, which had been retrofitted into a funeral home. Renovated from materials the undertaker had scavenged from old buildings targeted for demolition.

The hair on the back of his neck prickled, and goose bumps rose on his arms and legs. Plants in the windows had died and remained leafless in their pots. The brown and black Mortuary creaked and groaned even without the wind.

Unwillingly, Burt unbuckled his seat belt. He felt a chill run down his spine, causing him to shudder. Burt turned to open his door and came face to face with the dark-clad Undertaker. The Undertaker was a very tall, hawk-faced man with a handlebar mustache.

"I didn't mean to scare the death out of you, Officer, but I noticed your window was rolled down as you pulled up. Perhaps you're here to dig up some information, or are you just getting some dirt on a suspect?"

"How do you know I was coming to talk to you?"

"There are normally only one or two reasons someone would stop here. Either they are here to visit dead relatives or friends, or to be visited by a relative or friend. If you don't mind me saying so, you fit neither of those categories, at least not yet."

The Deputy grabbed the clipboard lying next to him on the seat. Nervously, he tapped it with his thumb. Sweat beaded on his upper lip and forehead.

"We have six names we would like you to look at. The Undertaker had to pull the clipboard out of Burt's hand to get a good look.

"Ah, yes, I know these names; they were all customers about a year ago. But surely the Sheriff knew this. After all, his wife's name is on the list?"

"The Sheriff is in no condition to think straight. Could you tell me what the six people have in common?"

"Well, they all died when the city's garbage truck lost control and plowed into Joseph's Corner Cafe. All six were killed instantly."

"Are they all buried in the cemetery?"

"Yes, side by side. Deputy, are you investigating their deaths or their lives?"

"What! What do you mean by their lives?" Burt wanted to leave, to pretend he had never come to this town. His six-month tenure in the police force had been quiet until now. Now, all hell was breaking loose. He wanted to leave Belchwater and never return. "Let me ask just one question. Were there any disturbances at the cemetery in the past few days?"

The Undertaker's voice interrupted his thoughts. "Were there any ghostly happenings in the city?"

"Until this morning, there hadn't been any disturbances for the last six months. Suddenly, these six people or whatever they are started harassing their families. I wouldn't have believed it if I hadn't seen it myself."

The Undertaker gave a grin as if he knew something. "The only disturbance here that I was aware of was the very loud parade yesterday. You know, to celebrate Memorial Day." The undertaker winked at the deputy with a crooked grin. "Deputy, let's take a ride in the cemetery?"

"With you?" Burt blurted out, embarrassed at his lack of control.

"We can take your car unless, of course, you would rather ride in the hearse?"

"Get in, and don't forget to buckle up."

Halfway through the cemetery, the Sheriff radioed. His wife had paid another visit with chicken soup. This time, she tried to feed him.

Frantically, he urged Burt to do something, anything. The Undertaker directed the deputy to the hills on the north end of the cemetery.

"The six graves are together on top of the hill. Slow down, Deputy, people are trying to rest around here."

"Well, people are trying to rest outside the cemetery as well." The two men stepped out of the car and walked toward the six graves. Burt followed the undertaker halfheartedly. The silence was overwhelming, even the birds weren't chirping.

Burt, unnerved, knew something or someone was waiting for them.

Suddenly, the sky grew dark, and the wind was howling. Dirt devils swirled all around them, kicking up dirt.

"Look," said the Undertaker. His long, narrow fingers were accented by the storm, which came out of nowhere. Lightning flashed and thunder rolled, echoing in Burt's ears.

Each of the six graves has a hole near where a headstone should be set. He looked in, motioning to the deputy to have a look.

"Oh boy, this is fun," Burt sighed. The officer had seen movies where a scared person had chattering teeth, but never thought it was possible. Until the moment he investigated the holes.

Looking down into the first hole, Burt could see the inside of the casket. Unsure of his faculties, he ran to the next grave, then the next, and the next.

"They're all empty, empty, but how?" He ran back to the car, leaning over the hood. Even the warmth of the engine didn't comfort him. Suddenly, lightning crashed into a nearby tree, showering cinders of red-hot wood across the car and Burt. He yelped as he stood to shake them off. Turning once again to face the Undertaker, they were so close they were almost touching faces.

"Stop that, you scared me to death."

"It would be a pleasure doing business with you. Deputy, did you notice there were no gravestones on any of the graves?"

"Now that you mention it, I did. But what does that have to do with anything?" Feeling a little weak and very puzzled, Officer O'Brien sat back in the seat of the patrol car. The Undertaker rushed into the passenger seat; he was full of life and energy. Burt was even more frightened now than before.

"This is exciting; I've heard of it but never actually seen it."

"Undertaker, what in the world are you talking about?"

"If a grave is left without a headstone, the site is unsealed. After a year, if the unsealed body is disturbed, a quickening takes place. In other words, the bodies come back to life."

Burt fidgeted in his seat, not sure he wanted to hear another word.

"The headstones have not been placed yet because the city hasn't settled on compensation for the accident."

"Politics stinks," murmured Burt.

"These bodies are tormenting their families due in part to the lack of a seal and secondly, because of the Memorial Day celebration. They think their families are glad they are dead. The problem being, the longer they inhabit this dimension of the living, leaving it will become harder and harder for the dead."

The police radio squelched, and then the voice of the Sheriff was heard. "Deputy, what's going on? Have you figured out what's happening? And where in the hell are you?"

"I'm on my way back to the mortuary, Sheriff. The Undertaker has it all figured out."

"Oh, he does, does he, well then how does he supposed to get rid of these walking corpses a second time?"

"Al, if your wife is around, watch what you say. It's possible she may become easily agitated." The Undertaker interrupted the conversation when he tapped the Deputy on the shoulder.

"Have the Sheriff contact all the families of the dead relatives, setting up a gathering at the cemetery. They will need to bring paint, boards, stakes, and a shovel. Oh, and Deputy, tell them to do it quickly, or it may be too late. So far, they haven't used any of the supernatural power in the

Higher plane dimension."

"Sheriff, the Undertaker says—."

"I heard him, and though it's hard to understand, I'm a believer in whatever is going on."

"I'm going to pick up some black robes at the mortuary so we can appear somber. What size do you wear, Deputy?"

As they pulled up, Burt was partially relieved to see some families were already present. Others arrived right after the deputy and undertaker. Six bodies flew over the cars, then hovered above the families as they approached the graves. The Sheriff's wife held a carving knife in one hand and a chicken in the other.

"Please, everybody, put on these robes and walk to the grave where your loved one is supposed to be buried," said the Undertaker.

"All right, now go on and do what the Undertaker told you," said Deputy O'Brien. "Not you, Mrs. Tate. We are wearing these for you." The elderly woman smiled slightly.

"Thank you, Deputy," said the Undertaker. "Now, if the families will paint the name of the dead family member on the wood and nail it to a stake, we will continue." The Undertaker went to each family and showed them what he meant.

The specters were raising cane as they flew between people and under their legs. Lightning again ignited the sky with blinding light, and echoing thunder cracked the silence with a deafening roar. "We also need a day of departure painted on the sign. A year ago, today."

"Sheriff, pound your head stone in and say something about how much you miss your wife." The older law enforcement officer slowly walked to the head of the grave. He wept and whispered as he pounded the stake into the head of the grave.

His wife screamed, flying high into the sky. Suddenly, she plummeted to the ground with the speed of a bullet, tearing into the ground, leaving only dust in her wake. One by one, the other families repeated the procedure until all the bodies were gone.

"I would fill in all the holes unless you want them to escape again." The Undertaker was solemn as he spoke his next words of caution. "Get some permanent headstones or the next time <u>you'll be in the soup</u>."
Dedicated To My Brother
David William Hazard

Ghost

Held to this earth
By chains of the past
Invisible by choice
Hidden from those who shouldn't see them
Seeing is believing
Appearing as a mist
Shadow
Feeling their cold chill as they pass by
Haunted themselves by memories
Often driven by them
Linked to souls left in life
Gentle as a cool breeze
Erupting violently when crossed
Watchers, guardians, tormenters, comforters
When the hairs prick the back of your neck
Your own personal ghost
Maybe protecting or haunting you

THE HAUNTING OF THE CAST IRON CAFÉ

The haunting of the Cast Iron Cafe is fictional and is only a figment of an overactive imagination. Of course, Halloween is around the corner, and who knows?

Doc Severn locked up the milk stop office, making a last-minute check to make sure everything was secure. He hoped to close early enough to get home and take his daughter Trudy trick-or-treating. People were coming into the milk stop, so Doc walked to the side entrance.

Entering the milk stop through the double doors, two men covered in sheets walked in. These two were assuming the role of ghosts. They cut holes in the sheets to see, and Doc could easily tell they were Caucasian.

"No trick or treating here, guys, and it appears you may be a little old anyway."

"We want green stuff for our treat pops, or you're going to get a real big trick."

"Now wait just a minute, I just closed shop, and the money was already deposited."

"Looks like trick time, old man."

"Will, is that you? I've got some cash. It's in my wallet. Doc reached for his wallet, and the two ghost thugs fired their shots as one, and the bullets tore Doc's gut and shoulder open. With a thud, he landed on the tile floor somewhere between life and death.

"Will, I will haunt you and this place forever."

"Clean out his wallet!" Will said.

Then Tommy whispered, "Let's drag him into the freezer and lock him in.

After moving the body, they cleaned up the blood trail on the floor. The Milk Stop was the last building on the way out or into town. So, the sleepy town of Coleman was unaware of the hideous crime that had taken place.

"Great said Doc, I'm going to die in the very room which almost took Trudie's life last year." She had been missing for an hour, and something told him to check the ice cream freezer. Inside was his daughter, freezing, but alive. "I guess the freezer finally claimed a victim."

Outside, the murderers were making their escape. "Hundred dollars weren't hardly worth the fuss."

"Oh, well, I've got to work on Monday, and Tommy, you gotta work tomorrow."

When Doc didn't get home that night, his wife called the police. The police went by the milk stop, and everything was locked up tight. Mrs. Severn was beside herself with worry; her husband had never been this late.

The next morning, Trudy heard her mom, Kathleen, crying. "Mommy, don't cry, Daddy told me he was in the ice cream place. You know the place he found me when I was so cold?"

"Sweetie, what do you mean, Daddy told you?"

"Mommy, Daddy was standing by my bed last night, and he told me he was sorry he missed trick or treat with me."

Kathleen. Trudy's mother called the police and told them to check the inside of the milk stop for Doc. "Please make sure to check the Ice Cream freezer."

Doc's lifeless body was sitting against the wall of the ice cream freezer. His eyes were open, and his right hand held his stomach, and his left hand lay at his side. Next to his right side on the floor, Doc had written in his own blood WT.

The policeman reached down to close Doc's eyes, and Doc's right hand clinched the policeman's hand and drew him in. Doc gasped in a raspy, far-away voice, "I will never leave here." The policeman jerked his arm away, and Doc fell over as dead as before. The policeman's partner saw the whole thing but was speechless. "Let's keep that out of the report."

After the funeral, the old Coleman Milk Stop resumed normal hours with William and Thomas resuming their jobs, though guilt shadowed them like a dark cloud. It wasn't long before windows were opening, and doors shutting without the help of human hands. At night, usually when the milk stop was closing, footsteps and banging noises were heard by all the employees.

One Thursday night, just a few minutes before closing, a customer asked for some Chocolate ice cream. Will got the chills in the freezer, and it wasn't the cold. To avoid the feeling of death, normally, he asked another employee to go into the freezer, but tonight he was alone. "Just a second he told the customer." He opened the door to the ice cream freezer, and it seemed even colder than normal. "Of course, he wanted chocolate; it was at the top," Will said to himself.

He stood on a chair to reach the tub of chocolate, and the chair shook, sending him to the floor, his arm snapped between the shoulder and the elbow. Before he could turn to run out the door, it shut, locking him in. With his good left hand, he pounded on the freezer door, but no one heard him. The customer miraculously vanished in a fog, and Wills' screams eventually stopped; and they found him dead the next morning.

Kathleen closed the Milk Stop, eventually selling it to a well-known Coleman Dairy, and a couple of the brothers reopened it seven years later. An ex-Milk Stop employee was hired to manage its operations.

Thomas wasn't too happy to be working in a place where his best friend had died, but he needed work. Everything seemed to be fine for the first year, and Thomas seemed to forget about his role in Doc's death and the murder of his friend Will. Then, around the middle of October, products were being moved from one place to another.

Doors opened and closed. Sometimes slamming or even locking themselves. Gallons of milk fell to the floor, breaking open and creating a mess on the walk-in floors. Outside the Milk Stop, the wind howled even when there was no wind. Thomas had started drinking to settle his nerves, drinking to laugh away the weird events unfolding before him. The owners found him passed out in the office with a bottle of Granddad in his hands, and they fired him.

Thomas, drunk out of his mind on Halloween night, decided to break some windows and doors at the milk stop around 11:45. He walked up to the front door ready to break it in with a bat when they opened.

"Is that the way you want to play, Doc? I'm not scared of you or anyone." He swaggered in the door, and they shut behind him. The lights flickered, and then Thomas heard laughter. Deep thundering laughter that continued until the lights went out. Everything was deathly quiet. Thomas got goosebumps as a chill swept over him. It was so cold, so fast, he couldn't move.

"How does the freezing cold feel, Tommy? This is how it felt all those years ago when you left me for dead." Tommy cried, and his tears froze on his cheeks. They were still frozen the next morning when they found him standing in the middle of the room, frozen. Not the freezer, just inside the milk processing room.

The Milk Stop closed for several years before a local man purchased it, renovating it into a drive-thru coffee shop. All the past deaths and hauntings were never discussed, and in 1999, the former milk stop was now called the "Cast Iron Cafe."

A few years after opening, it was decided to turn part of the building into a winery. The first year's wine turned out to be a success, and so the second year started, and Doc reared his ugly head. Barrels of wine were knocked off their stands. The large holding tanks were opened, spilling gallons of wine down the floor drains.

The owner and manager decided to have a meeting after the shop closed one night. They began discussing the things happening around the shop. Suddenly, lights began to flicker, and doors began opening and shutting on their own. Then they heard fingernails scraping a chalkboard, which made both men shudder. When they looked at the chalkboard, there was a message written on it. "No more wine, sell milk."

The wine was dumped, and the Cast Iron Cafe expanded into a coffee roastery and a place where milk could once again be purchased by customers driving through. Not just milk, but eggs, half-and-half too. It seemed that since coffee and milk had a sort of symbiotic relationship, Doc let it go. The haunting stopped, and the Cast Iron Cafe has become a permanent fixture in Coleman.

Well, the haunting hasn't completely stopped; it only happens on All Hallows' Eve. That's when Doc gets to give the employees of the Cafe some scares and excitement. Oh yeah, and as soon as it gets dark on Halloween night, whip cream bottles pop open, the lights flicker, while the wind laughs as it howls through the old building. As you drive through at night, the reflection you see in the doors and windows may not be your own, but that of a middle-aged man pointing his finger at you as you pass by. Trudy, even though no longer a spring chicken enjoys her father's Halloween bantering.

Happy Halloween! And remember, Trick or Treat.

Dreams

Late-night ice cream
Undigested food
A scary dream that makes you scream
Some romantic
Others are abstract or surreal
Usually seen in monochromatic
There are those who inform of innermost thoughts
Streaming dreams from the founts of the heart
Intensity flowing from loveless droughts
Nightmares awaken from deep sleep
Foretelling of future demise
Haunting feelings that make you weep
Joy or sorrow are the games of dreams
Take either too seriously
Coaxing our imagination, it seems

I'M ALWAYS WATCHING

"Thomas, I had a terrible dream last night."

"Yeah, me too, but I don't remember it." Her husband sat down at the table to await his breakfast. Normally, she didn't mind serving him a hearty breakfast, but this morning she wanted a little more interest from Thomas.

"Here's your eggs," Florence said with a huff. "Over easy, just like you want them. Your toast will be ready in just a few minutes."

"You mean it's not ready yet? How am I supposed to sop up the yoke when it runs?" Thomas said with a grin.

She tried to ignore his attempt at humor and shot him a glare. Florence walked to the tiled counter and waited for the toast to pop up. Thirty seconds later, the toast was dumped on her husband's plate on top of his half-eaten eggs.

"Hey, what in the heck are you doing?"

"When someone tells you they've had a bad dream, you're supposed to ask them what it was."

Instead of asking the question, he merely mentioned that the eggs were good. Florence sat down next to him, sipping her cup of Joe.

"I dreamt I was at my funeral in Wisconsin. There was a nice turnout, most of them were family. But part of my immediate family was missing, and the other two were asleep. It was as if I were outside my body looking at my body and those around me."

"Look, Darling, it was just a dream. Don't let it ruin your day." Florence was thinking about their upcoming trip to celebrate her grandparents' 50th anniversary. The kids and grandkids were getting together to work on their home.

"Thomas, if something happens to me while we're on our vacation, there are two things I want you to promise. Enroll the kids at St.

Anthony's school, and if things get hairy, please let my mother help with the kids."

"Florence, stop talking about death, funerals, out of body experiences. Just drop the whole thing."

"Promise me, Thomas, and I'll drop it."

"All right, all right, I promise."

"Good, would you like another cup of coffee?"

"No, I think I'd better go to work."

Later that day, Florence called her mom.

"Mom, I want to talk to you about a dream I had last night."

"Would you like to talk about it over the phone or would you like me to come over?"

"I believe it would be best for you to come over."

"Okay, I'll be there around lunch."

Florence hung up the phone and walked around the new house they had recently moved into. "What a shame I won't be alive to enjoy it in my old age."

"Mom, it was so real."

"Now listen here, dreams are not the foreshadowing of the future events which will shape our lives, merely pictures randomly developed in the mind. I've heard if you eat ice cream before you go to sleep, you'll have wild dreams."

"Well, I didn't have any ice cream, and there's just something about the dream coupled with a feeling I have that there is impending doom ahead."

"Listen, Flo, stop talking nonsense. You have a great car, a new home, three lovely children, and a good husband."

"I know, Mom. If something were to happen to me, and Thomas had problems with the children, would you help?"

"I would rather drop the subject."

"Yes, but that doesn't answer the question."

"Of course. Now I must get back to work. I'll see you later, honey."

For days, then weeks, Florence felt heaviness within herself. A foreboding presence engulfed her more with each passing moment. Thomas walked away every time she mentioned the word dream.

The torment started to wear away at her normally easy-going spirit. The nightmare was not only ruling but also disrupting life. She decided to ignore it, the way everyone was beseeching her to do. Her family needed her more than ever. Flo clutched the gold cross which dangled from around her neck, whispering words to heaven.

School was about to end, and Craig, her seven-year-old, was having difficulty in school. Between the baby, daughter Lisa, and her dread of late, Craig hadn't had the attention he was used to. Florence decided to enter him in Vacation Bible School for the whole two-week program. After which, they would start their vacation.

She longed to visit her grandmother in Madison and, hopefully, see her sister's family in Tennessee. She didn't believe she would make it that far. Yet there was always hope.

The week before school was out, her son Craig came to the table in the dining room to see what she was doing. At first, he seemed puzzled.

"Mommy, why are our names on that paper you put in your wallet?"

"It's in case something happens to us while we are on vacation. If anybody finds us, they will know who you children are, and who to contact in case of emergency."

"Who will they contact, Mommy?"

"Your Grandma Bencraft?"

"Are we going to have an accident?"

"No, but it's always a good idea to be ready in case anything happens. She couldn't look her son in the eye. Flo wasn't even sure she believed her answer. Now, why don't you go out and play in the back yard?" She didn't want her son to worry his young life away.

Florence realized she didn't even believe what she had told her son; she must keep her doubt out of her family's minds. No, it was best to keep it to herself and let life stay on its course. She had done everything in her power to be prepared, so it was time to live. Life carried on normally for the next three weeks. Thomas flushed the radiator and engine, with Craig right under his feet every step of the way. Craig stepped on a bee, and his foot swelled so much he couldn't wear a shoe for three days of Vacation Bible School.

The last day of Vacation Bible School is ending. The station wagon was packed, and the family loaded except for Craig, who they picked up on their way out of town. So, a nervously anticipated cross-country trek from California to Wisconsin began.

Without stopping longer than an hour at any time, the Hamilton family was making good time. Craig had a dream during the night that woke him from his sleep. He told his mom about the dream. "We were in a crash, and the car tumbled. Things were flying everywhere, and then I woke up."

His dad raised his voice, "No more talk of dreams for the rest of our trip." Then, in the rear-view mirror, he saw his father, listening.

Craig didn't say another word, even though he kept seeing a strange reflection in the passenger-side window, which kept reminding him of his dream. He didn't want to bother his parents, especially his father, so he kept it to himself.

On the morning of the third day, they stopped for breakfast at a roadside cafe. After a quick bite, Thomas loaded up the family and began driving the long, tedious highway through Wyoming.

Florence snickered as Craig told his father to beat the car in front of them. Her fear of death had vanished, and she was enjoying her worry-free road trip.

Without warning, the car swerved, and she was hurled out the passenger side window to the shoulder of the road. The last thing she remembered was a sudden feeling of flight as she looked down at her body, which was being rolled over by the station wagon. The wheels kept her from being squished.

Her last word before she passed away, "Craig."

Thomas pulled the children from the wreck and laid them on the side of the road. Craig awoke to see an ambulance leaving the scene and another pulling up. His dad carried Lisa to the ambulance, and Craig followed close on his heels. Daniel, the baby was being strapped in."

"Craig, you make sure your brother and sister don't fall out." A task to take his son's mind off what had happened. Thomas sat in front with the ambulance driver.

The emergency room was hurriedly checking out Thomas and the two oldest kids. Daniel was in intensive care with a head injury. The next day, Craig and Lisa visited their father in his room. "Where is Mom?" asked Craig. "In the basement," answered a solemn father. Ending the conversation, as the nurse said, their father needed to sleep.

The grandparents came to take the children on the train from Rock Springs, Wyoming, to Madison, Wisconsin.

The small church was full, with only a few empty seats strung throughout the sanctuary. Florence looked in the handsome coffin only to see herself lying with her hands crossed within. People walked by and looked at her. Many with tears running down their cheeks and still others saying things she knew they wished they'd said at an earlier time.

A little boy with blond hair slowly made his way to the coffin. Florence knew the boy as her son, Craig. He wasn't his normal happy, radiant self. His face was expressionless, his eyes empty. He walked limply, staring at the lifeless body he knew as his mother. "How could she look so pretty when she was squished by a car?" He said to himself. His mother could hear his thoughts. Craig was thinking of horny toads he'd seen that had been run over on the side of the road.

Everyone took their seats, and the minister spoke eloquently, consoling those who felt the loss of a special person who now walks in a higher, joyful realm.

Florence looked in the front row of the sanctuary and stared in disbelief. She realized her dream had come full circle. Before her, there were two empty chairs. Next to the empty chairs slumped Craig and Lisa, asleep on each other's shoulders. Thomas and Daniel were absent, and the rest of her family and friends listened to the minister as she exited through the open beam ceiling, answering the call of sudden jealousy. In an instant, she is in a home in Rock Springs, Wyoming, peering down on her husband, who is intimately getting to know a nurse from the hospital.

Her anger grew, and she screamed. The window above the sex filled bed shattered outward. The bed was shaking, lifted into the air, then dropped.

The room shook with the power of her anger.

"I'm not even in the grave yet, and you're nursing your little brain." Both Thomas and the nurse heard Florence's voice. Thomas rolled off the nurse and onto the floor. The nurse pulled the sheet over her head as tightly as she could. Floating above her husband, Florence appeared to him as one highly pissed off angel.

"You should get back to the hospital and be with our son. You bring our family home and protect them. I'll be there watching."

Thomas was already putting his pants on and making his way to the door. As he exited the house, there was a blood-curdling scream, and the door slammed behind him, shattering the glass windows on either side of the door jam. His back was pelted with small glass shards.

"This is your warning, remember your promise, Thomas, or I'll be back sending you to the afterlife." True to her words, Florence guarded her family, peering into their rooms at night. So far, Thomas has kept his promise, so far.

Dedicated To All Dreamers

Witches

Hidden within the depths of the forest
Always planning evil, no time to rest
Toads, black cats, and bats are all about
Potions made with the ear of a pig and a bear's snout
A recluse in a secluded hideaway
Always ready to fly with no desire to stay
Inside the ramshackle shack
Fires burning under caldrons, black
Hundreds of candles floating around
The witches cackle, the only sound
Words from a mystic book read aloud
Smoke clinging to the ceiling in a shroud
Black and silver-streaked hair, shiny and flat
Crooked nose and pointy hat
The blue moon rises on a cloudless night
Ready to fill men's hearts with fright

SCARED FATHER

Just the other day, I received a letter from my father that sent chills down my spine. After I read it, I didn't go out after dark for a week.

This is how it read:

Greetings from your scared father. A funny, ha-ha thing happened to me three nights ago as I was closing the ranch. The night was already eerie. There wasn't a single thing that put me out of sorts; it was a culmination of everything. The ocean seemed restless, and the waves hit the nearby beach louder than usual.

A boisterous wind blew leaves, swayed trees, and howled at the full moon. I was down by the barn when it happened. Now, son, I know you may want to laugh, but you weren't there, and I was. As I walked next to the big barn, I wished I had just gone into the house and gone to sleep. Like I said, I was locking everything up like every other night.

As I rounded the front of the barn, I realized how beautiful the moon was that evening. It seemed larger than normal and very bright. As I drew closer to the barn doors, the wind became stronger. Branches from leafless trees creaked as they swayed in harmony with each gust. An owl watched me pass his roost, and he hooted, almost as if he was warning me not to go in the barn.

The hair on the back of my neck was prickling, and a cold shiver ran down my spine, like someone or something was standing on my grave. Reaching out to open the barn doors, but stopped short when the eerie cackle of an old woman echoed from within the building. It is the first time I have ever had goosebumps.

I shoved on the barn doors, and they wouldn't open. The harder I pulled and pushed on the doors, the louder the laughter became. There was movement inside, then singing.

Heckling pot so black and round

Mix with bubbles a glorious sound

Make a mixture, magical tonight

Give my broom the gift of flight
To scare all those below my feet
To steal their souls, my greatest treat.

Clouds rolled in front of the moon, engulfing the ranch in blackness. My blood ran cold. "Come out, we don't allow the homeless or fires in the barn." There was no answer at first, just silence. Then a sigh followed by a long-drawn-out groan. Dropping my flashlight, I turned to run to the house and call the police.

The barn doors burst open behind me, followed by a blood-curdling, high-pitched scream. Turning again towards the large barn, the smell of burnt wood and blood turned my legs into rubber, and I almost fell. Though I wanted to run away, I was compelled to go forward.

The horse stalls were on the left, and the ranch equipment was on the right. The first stall was empty, and the second. I was ready to grab anything that might come at me. Suddenly, something jumped on my back, making terrible noises. It clawed my back, and pain gripped me. In terror, I tripped over myself and landed on the floor. Whatever was on me took off towards the barn doors. The clouds had gone, and the moon shone bright. Bright enough to see the ranch cats exiting the barn.

I was relieved and angry at myself for being so scared. Getting up on my feet, it was time to investigate the rest of the barn. On the far end of the barn was a small fire with a huge cast-iron pot. The head of a horse sticking out. The horse seemed to be talking to a shadowy figure standing beside the cauldron. The horse looked at me, and I knew it was Solomon, one of our Arabians.

"Bob, you shouldn't be here," the horse's head said.

The shadowy figure turned towards me with faint yellow eyes piercing what courage I had left. Then, with a cackle and a blood-curdling scream, the figure flew at me so fast I barely had the time to jump out of the way.

Back and forth the creature flew, keeping me pinned to the ground. Rolling to my back and frozen by a witch hovering over me on an old broom. "Well, Robert, son of Alfred and Ruth, it's time for me to go. Tonight is your lucky night. You live till next we meet, if you're still here next All Hallow's Eve, you'll be the trick and my treat."

This land has been my haunt since I left Salem. You should find another to call home. Unless you want to ride Solomon in the afterlife." Without hesitation, she flew out of the barn, cackling until she had gone. The barn was unharmed, and only Solomon was gone, along with the caldron and any evidence of foul play.

"Son, this happened three nights ago. I'm still trying to wrap my head around everything that happened. We are moving as soon as possible, hopefully before Halloween. If you don't hear from me after that, be careful not to kill or harm any cats or mice or horses, I guess. JUST IN CASE!"

Signed your scared father.

My sisters mentioned that Dad must have gone on vacation. Neither of them had heard from him since October 31st. Two weeks later, I received another letter from my dad...

"How are you doing? We just got two new horses to keep Solomon happy. Did you like my story? Hope it was scary enough for you? It's about time the storyteller got STORIED."

"Ha, ha, ha!"
Dedicated to my Dad,
Robert W. Hazard

ZOMBIES

Friends, we hung out with
Loved ones, we held and kissed
Now strangers, enemies, and murderers
The blame is not theirs
Even so, they must die
Dead but not dead
Bitten to die, living undead
Attracted to noise
Slow thinking, slow moving
Eyes white
skin deteriorating
The appearance of spiderwebs
From blackened vessels under thinning skin
Always driven by hunger
They advance
Some missing arms or legs
Walking, limping, and dragging themselves
Ever closer towards their prey
Brains to eat
Brains are their Achilles' heel
A headshot to a Zombie is mercy
All the good Zombies are dead zombies.

ZOMBIES AFOOT

The university in Juneau wasn't large, yet well-funded by outside sources. They have a research wing dedicated to the development of a healing salve, or at least that's the cover story.

The Department of Defense was working on debilitating agents to wipe out other armies or terrorists. They also wanted a neutralizing agent to counteract its effects. These scientists were trying to use more natural or naturally occurring agents.

Graduate students who had been paid to participate in clinical trials entered the research wing of the campus. Students participating in the trials were supposedly transferred to other universities with full scholarships.

The research team was ready to try a more radical aerosol agent derived from the brown recluse spider. The synthesized venom was forced into spray cans under great pressure.

The healing agent was synthesized from Saint Bernard saliva enzymes enhanced with a cocktail of antibiotics. Though a bit rushed, the results were positive.

Lambert was the next on the trial list and was waiting in the examining room for his test to begin. A mediocre student, barely squeaking by. His payment for participating in the trials was passing grades and then graduating with his peers. His only goal was to take his small gang of motorcycle buddies and raise havoc in Juneau. Of course, with his girl Winnie sitting right behind him.

Lambert was under the impression he was trying a new sunscreen, SPF 300. They had him wear a Speedo for greater skin exposure. The doctor came in and asked how he was doing. "Great, can we just get this show on the road?"

"Of course," The researcher replied. "My name is Sean; I'll be helping you today. Here you are, now add a little to your skin and let's see how it interacts with your chemistry."

Lambert grabbed the can out of the doctor's hands and started to spray the contents on his arms. It immediately began to burn, and he threw the can against the floor, and it exploded. The deep red gas engulfed both men instantly, and their screams were heard throughout the complex.

The other researchers were watching in another room. "Oh my God, release the healing serum!" One of the researchers pushed a large red button, and the examining room was flooded with a blue gaseous cloud. The screams diminished, and the men passed out in exhaustion.

After the examination room had been cleared of biohazards, the other researchers entered the room and were shocked at what they saw. Lambert was worse because of the exposure to the brown recluse toxin. Both had necrotizing ulcers. Lambert's body was covered with 90 percent of open lesions. The researcher estimated approximately 20 percent. Both men seemed to be healing from the outer part of the legions towards the center.

Most of their ears and noses were eaten away, along with a few fingertips, which were dissolving on the floor. Black eyes filled their sockets like giant pupils.

"How are you feeling?" one of the technicians asked.

Both Lambert and the injured technician opened their mouths, and nothing came out. Within were shriveled tongues and burnt throats damaged beyond healing.

They isolated each patient in separate rooms and began rigid monitoring. After just a few hours, both men were healing rapidly. The lesions on their skin were all gone except for marbled discoloration, and blood vessels swelling to three or four times normal. seemingly spreading. Their eyes were mutating into multiple pupils, and their communication was limited to moans.

After 8 hours, their skin appeared to be tightening to their skeletal substructure. They were extremely thirsty. The two patients were being transferred to Area 75, a secret location.

Lambert waved a researcher over and pointed at his throat. The woman leaned over, "Open your mouth and let me have a look." Without warning, Lambert pulled the researcher in and ripped her throat open, drinking the blood gushing out as fast as he could. As she died, Lambert moaned, dropping her like a rag doll to the floor.

He could see multiples of everything yet instinctively knew exactly what he was looking at. His thirst was unquenchable, but lessened from the lady drink he just finished.

In another room, Sean was getting every scan the facility had available. He was getting all the help while Lambert was a Guinea pig. Though healed on the outside with permanent discoloration, he was dissolving on the inside. His eternal organs were melting at a rate giving him about 7 days to live.

His blood work revealed the Brown recluse venom was multiplying internally while neutralized externally. The healing agent derived from Saint Bernard's saliva only affected what it adhered to. They tried to inject the healing serum into the patients' bloodstream, but it was rejected, and the patient went into cardiac arrest and seemed to die.

Lambert burst into the room and lunged at the nearest researcher, ripping his throat open. The supposed dead Sean leapt from his bed, grabbing the other lab tech, also ripping at her throat and then drinking from a spurting fountain of blood.

As they exited the room, others in the facility screamed, running from the creatures, slowly making their way to an exit. There were a couple of brave employees who tried to stop them. Lambert and Sean were no longer in pain. Their nerves were decimated from the recluse venom, allowing them no physical restraint.

Students and employees were running from the college, screaming, "Zombies, real live, almost dead zombies." Lambert and Sean were now hunting in different directions. Lambert was heading into the city, and Sean towards the security guard who had pulled his pistol and readied himself for a confrontation. "Stop, I'm Officer Krankle. You look like a brainless Zombie, so I will aim for your head."

Sean walked at a steady pace towards the security guard without hesitation, no signs of stopping. "This is your last chance, please stop!" Sean advanced and was within 10 feet of Krankle. The Security Guard fired, missing the first time, and Sean was almost within striking distance. He fired again, and the bullet entered the forehead with brain matter, which followed the bullet as it exited. Sean crumpled to the ground, releasing fluids trapped in his body in a massive bloody puddle.

Immediately, three researchers from the laboratory were on the scene. "We will take care of this. There is another one heading into town." Krankle looked at the two women and the man, "What happened to him?"

"He was bitten by a dozen or so Brown Recluse spiders."

"There are no poisonous spiders in Alaska."

"They were part of an exhibit on loan from California," one of the researchers said. "Maybe instead of a hundred questions, you should try to find the other one."

"Yeah, alright," Krankle called the Juneau Police and informed them of the situation. I'll radio in with updates as soon as I have some."

So far, there was a trail of dead bodies to follow. You would think that when people saw a person getting their throat ripped out and blood gushing out, they would run. But instead, they had to be lookie-loos and set themselves up to be the next victims.

The last victim was around the corner from the mall. Krankle guessed Lambert went to the mall to get some fast food. He entered the main doors expecting a blood bath, but everything inside was normal.

Around the corner and a block away, Lambert was walking down the street where his girlfriend Winnie lived. Winnie saw him walking up to the house, and she rushed out to jump into his arms. From a distance, he was her Lamby, but up close, he was not the ruggedly handsome young man she knew. He held up his arms to hug her, though he was very thirsty, he still knew he wanted Winnie in his life.

Her dude had skin and bones with blue, red, purple, and yellow blotches all over his body. His once deep blue eyes were now eyes made up of several black ones. There was blood all over him and huge pieces of flesh hanging from his teeth. She allowed him to hug her, but he smelled like death, and she had to pull away. "What happened to you, Lamby?" She grabbed his hand, guiding him into the house with his left foot dragging.

Pointing to his throat and moaning, Winnie understood he couldn't speak. Out of a kitchen drawer, she grabbed a pad and pen for Lambert to write on. He was fighting a tremendous thirst, but concentrated on writing down what happened to him. He wrote until the gist of the whole situation was written out, and then he handed her the pad to read.

She looked at him with sad, compassionate eyes and took her phone off the counter. "I'm calling Meals on Wheels to get you some thirst-quenching blood. Don't worry, I am here with you to the end." She dialed, and a man answered. "Hey, Tony, how about you come over and we have some fun?" As she set the phone down, she said, "After you feed, I want you to make love to me, while you still can."

When Lambert had entered the room where the lab rats were tending to their friend, he heard them saying he only had 7 days to live. He realized that because he was exposed to a greater extent, his time might even be shorter. Now Winnie knew that, too. Winnie was the one thing in life he was passionate about; he regretted that he would not have a life beyond this week with her.

Tony pulled up in front of the house and checked himself in his rear-view mirror, "Looking good, my man." Winnie met him at the door and led him into the kitchen. Lambert sprang from the pantry, taking Tony by surprise, ripping out his throat. Drinking until Tony lay empty and twitching on the floor.

"Good riddance, I couldn't stand him." Lambert managed to smile accompanied by a long moan. "My family is visiting Anchorage for two weeks, so we have the place to ourselves. She led him to her parents' bedroom and the massive Cal King, which was calling their names.

Lambert was happy his Speedo had protected at least that part of his body he would need to make Winnie happy. Hopefully, it will be an experience she will never forget. Though he and Winnie had never gone that far before, and he was excited, he was also very thirsty. How long could he go without tearing her throat open?

Thirty minutes later, she rolled off him as he pointed to his mouth and moaned and moaned. Scared he might just come after her, she ran to the kitchen and called Monique. "Hey, Monique, why don't you come over and we will go to the mall and do some shoe shopping."

Lambert was right behind her as she turned from her phone call. "In just a few minutes, someone will be here to quench your thirst. Then I am going to go to the mall to shop for shoes, and you can drink from a smorgasbord of blood fountains.

Since Lambert hadn't shown up at the mall for over an hour, Krankle went back to the research facility at the college. An obvious clean-up/ cover-up was underway, and Krankle suspected it was more like a cover-up. "What were the names of the two men who left this facility on a killing rampage?" The receptionist shrugged her shoulders, "Nobody has left this facility in the last 7 hours. In about an hour, our shift change, then people will be in and out."

"Look," said Krankle. "I shot one of your researchers two hours ago, about three hundred yards from here. Your fellow employees already talked to me." Krankle could see the receptionist was scared and worried. "There is still a killer out there, and I want to find him before he kills repeatedly. I need his name."

She leaned in and said, "Danny Lambert is a fourth-year student."

"Thank you," Krankle replied as he sped off to the College admin office. Once in the office, he found that many of the students in and out of the office knew Lambert. He had a girlfriend named Winnie who lived about a block from the mall. "That's where he went," The guard said under his breath. Krankle high-tailed it to the zombie's girlfriend's residence.

He found a yellow house with brick red trim. There were two cars parked in front, and one of them still had a warm engine. Cautiously, he walked up to the front door. It was open a few inches, so he drew his pistol and quietly walked into the first room, the kitchen. Before he got there, he smelled the iron smell of what he supposed was blood.

On the floor, side by side, were the bodies of a young woman and a man. Both with their necks ripped open and drained of blood. He called 911, then the police department to get the cavalry to the mall, where Krankle was sure Lambert was headed to kill more prey. From all appearances, he killed his girlfriend and the other young man just to try and quench some unfathomable thirst. A thirst that seemed to be non-ending.

He got to the mall at the same time as the police. Just as they were leaving their squad cars, the doors of the mall burst open, and a crowd emerged screaming and tripping over each other to escape. Krankle stopped a couple and asked what was going on.

"There's a Zombie in there, and he's tearing people's necks open and drinking their blood."

"Where is he?"

"He's eating or drinking in the food court. Let go of us!"

Krankle and two of the Juneau police force entered the mall slowly, heading for the food court. "He will appear as a Zombie, maybe he's not, but don't take any chances. If you see him shoot the monster in the head," Krankle explained as they neared the area where Lambert was killing.

Screams diminished, but the scene was horrific. Lambert was a messy eater with blood and twitching warm bodies littering the mall.

A human-looking creature headed towards them. He was discolored and dragging one foot behind. Moaning with every step as he slowly closed the distance between himself and the two police officers. He was close enough for the men to see huge pieces of flesh dangling from his teeth. Blood was still gurgling in his throat.

They aimed at the creature and fired center mass, and it rocked Lambert from side to side. He walked on like it didn't even feel it. A young woman ran out of the shoe store screaming, "Don't hurt him. Lamby is my boyfriend." Distracted, the first officer looked at Winnie, then back to Lambert just in time to have his neck ripped open. Lambert wasn't worried about anything but drinking.

The sound of a pistol firing caused Lambert to look up, and Winnie began to scream, "No!" Lambert's head exploded, and he crumpled to the ground, lifeless on top of the dead officer. The other officer grabbed Winnie and placed her in handcuffs.

Krankle walked over, "I'm sorry you had to die. I'm just glad you're not like a real zombie, or we would be in serious trouble right now." Winnie seemed to cramp up and fell to the ground. She threw up and felt her tummy move.

"Oh, Lambert, thank you for the gift." Under her breath, so no one else could hear, "I'll make sure and take good care of our baby." She rubbed her stomach and smiled.

Richard A. Hazard

Don't miss out!

Visit the website below and you can sign up to receive emails whenever Richard A Hazard publishes a new book. There's no charge and no obligation.

https://books2read.com/r/B-A-EZFAB-ETBYC

BOOKS2READ

Connecting independent readers to independent writers.

About the Author

Richard began writing songs at the age of twelve. Then in his teenage years to calm himself, he began to write poetry. Richard made up stories daily to exercise his and his families imagination. An imagination which would be his instrument to wield the world of fiction.

Bedtime stories for his children and grandchildren, have been written down and saved. His wife Nilah has finally convinced him to illustrate these stories and publish them for other children to enjoy.

With his family as his muse, Richard hopes to continue story telling for years.